Santa's Slip Up

by Raven Howell

Santa's Slip Up by Raven Howell

Published by Pen It Publications in the U.S.A.

713-526-3989

www.penitpublications.com

ISBN: 978-1-63984-463-0

Illustrated by: Savannah Horton

If it wasn't the cat
on the purple mat,

nor night wind's whistle and moan,

nor the skeleton creaking and
clunking about,

nor the dog busy
chewing his bone,

If it wasn't the spider
in a spinning web slider,

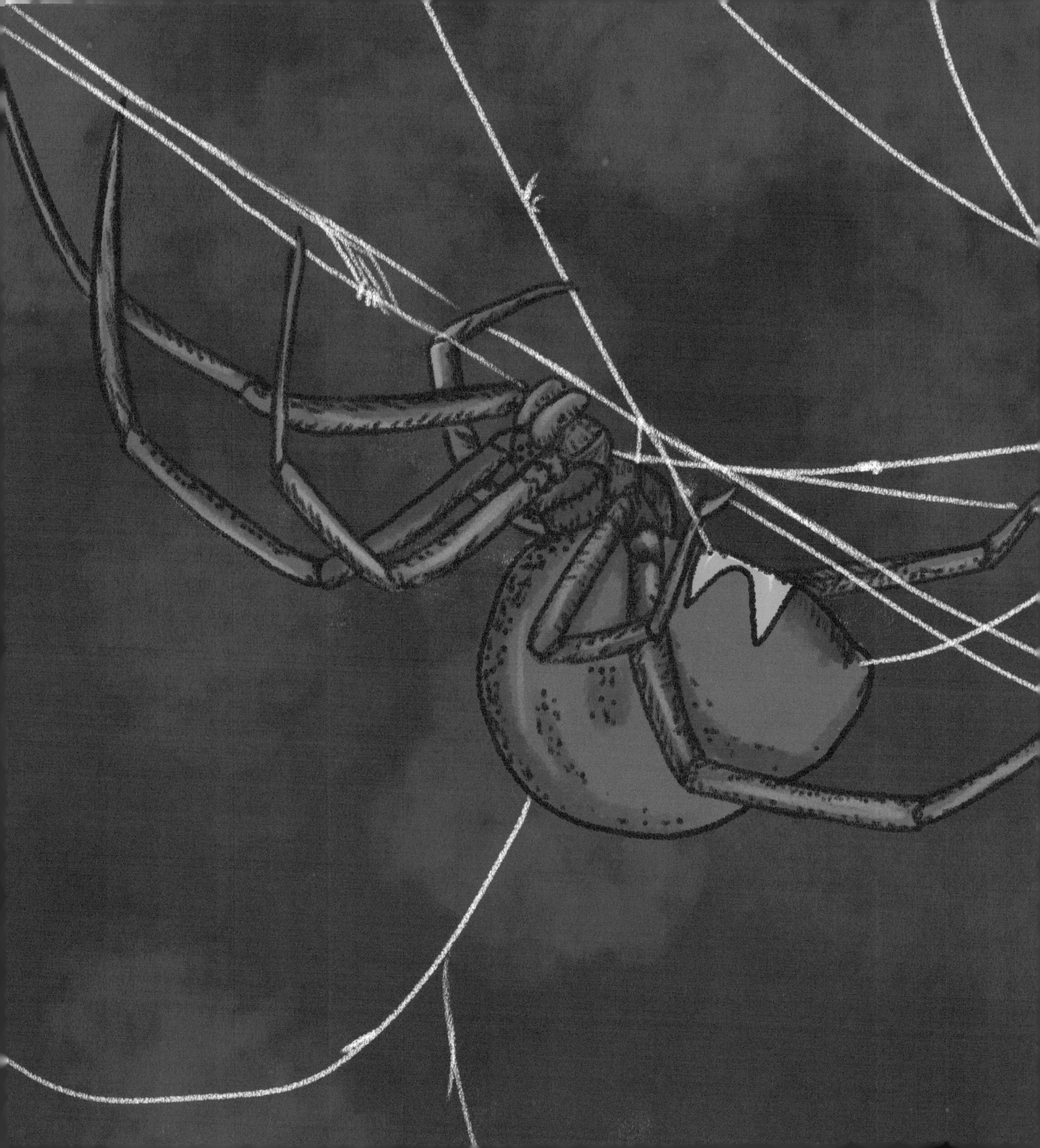

nor the bats hung in
trees, upside down,

If it wasn't the creepy
glow-in-the-darks,

nor the uncanny, spine-
chilling clown...

If it wasn't the ghost

who was nibbling his
toast,

nor the wart-on-the-
nose bossy witch,

If it wasn't the owl
with his hoot song and
scowl,

nor the zombie who
rambled and twitched,

If it wasn't the moon
round as a balloon,

nor the vampire, nor the
black crow,

If it wasn't the hobbling,
groaning goblin,

then who cheered,

Merry Christmas! Ho-ho!?

Merry Christmas!

Oops.

What a puzzling sight

on Halloween night

to see Santa in wintry
cheer.

With twinkling eyes,

St. Nick showed surprise,

"Oops! I came the wrong time
of the year!"

But no one that evening,

only skeletons thieving,

only dog, crow, the witch,
clown, and bat,

No one but the zombie, creepy-
crawly, and goblin,

no one, but the spider and cat,

Nada one but the ghost and
the vampire host

knew Santa was not in
disguise.

Yet in funny charade,

Santa joined the parade

and he won the year's Best
Costume prize.

PARADE
1st.

About the Author

Raven Howell writes stories and poetry for children. Having published several award-winning picture books, she enjoys sharing her love of literature by visiting classrooms and libraries. Raven is Creative & Publishing Advisor for *Red Clover Reader*, Poetry Director for *Monster Magnificent*, and writes *The Book Bug* column for *Story Monsters Ink* magazine. Her poems are found in children's magazines such as *Ladybug, Spider, Highlights for Children, Humpty Dumpty,* and *Hello Magazine*. She's a Collaborating Author for *Reading is Fundamental SoCal*.

Raven delights in sunshine, a good mystery, music, spending time with her family, and laughing. She's a huge fan of Santa Claus, and warm butterscotch chocolate chip cookies.

Excited to share *Santa's Slip Up*, Raven hopes to inspire readers in making the best of any situation one may find themselves in!